Rowan Coleman lives with her husband and five children in a very full house in Hertfordshire. She juggles writing novels with raising her family, which includes a very lively set of toddler twins whose main hobby is going in opposite directions. When she gets the chance, Rowan enjoys sleeping, sitting and loves watching films; she is also attempting to learn how to bake.

Rowan would like to live every day as if she were starring in a musical, although her daughter no longer allows her to sing in public. Despite being dyslexic, Rowan loves writing, and has written twelve novels, including her *Sunday Times* bestseller *The Memory Book* which was part of the Richard and Judy Autumn Book Club, and the award-winning *Runaway Wife*.

www.rowancoleman.co.uk

Facebook/Twitter: @rowancoleman

D0280152

ROWAN COLEMAN

Looking for Captain Poldark

EBURY
PRESS

1 3 5 7 9 10 8 6 4 2

Ebury Press, an imprint of Ebury Publishing
20 Vauxhall Bridge Road,
London SW1V 2SA

Penguin
Random House
UK

Ebury Press is part of the Penguin Random House group of companies
whose addresses can be found at global.penguinrandomhouse.com

First published in 2017 by Ebury Press

www.penguin.co.uk

A CIP catalogue record for this book is available from the British Library

ISBN 9781785033186

Typeset in India by Thomson Digital Pvt Ltd, Noida, Delhi

Printed and bound in Great Britain by Clays Ltd, St Ives PLC

Penguin Random House is committed to a sustainable future for our
business, our readers and our planet. This book is made from Forest
Stewardship Council® certified paper.

MIX
Paper from
responsible sources
FSC® C018179

CHATER ONE

* *

LISA

Location: 23 (a) Parker Street, Leeds

Radio station: Aire FM

Track playing: 'I Want to Dance with Somebody' by Whitney Houston

Miles travelled: 0

Miles until Captain Poldark: 543.5

Lisa closed her front door – hard enough to hear the click of the latch – and then turned the deadlock key. She heard the reassuring clunk of the bolt slide into place. She pushed against the door once, twice and a final third time. She then crossed it off her list in her notebook.

'This is it,' she said aloud into the quiet calm summer morning. Standing on her doorstep, she took a moment to notice how beautiful Parker Street was – at least when there were no other people in it, cluttering it up with their lives.

Lisa reached her tired but reliable little lilac Nissan Micra. She checked in the back seat, as she always did, just to make sure there were no axe-murderers waiting to pounce. Of course Lisa knew in her rational mind that the chances of there being an axe-murderer waiting in the back of her Micra were slim to none. However, she still had to check.

At some point, some years ago, Lisa had become very frightened of almost everything. She wasn't just frightened of axe-murderers and terrorists or war or an outbreak of an unstoppable zombie virus. She was also terrified of her next-door neighbour, the guy who got the bus every morning at the stop across the road, old Mrs Rashid in the corner shop, the checkout girl in Asda . . . pretty much everyone and everything she could think of. And Lisa spent a great deal of time thinking of new things to be afraid of. She reasoned, in a very unreasonable way, that if she could think of it, then it might not actually happen.

Lisa knew that most 'normal' people would think of her as really very odd. But knowing that didn't seem to help at all. It could be worse, she often thought to herself. You could be mad, and *not* know it.

And then she'd wondered if actually that wouldn't be better.

As it was, there was only one way Lisa had found to get by from day to day without spending it under her bed. This was to check and double check, secure and triple-secure her life in every single way she could think of. Otherwise she would be gripped by terror that seemed just as real to her as her bedside table, or the pot plant she'd inherited from her mum. However, the effort to try and keep herself safe meant that – up until today at least – she spent most of her time locked in her house, her own prisoner.

Keeping the world out was the only thing that worked, and reading books helped too. In books Lisa became a hundred, a *thousand* different people, who were all more brave, more clever and more beautiful than she. They were people who had a future, people who had a happy ending. She had thought that perhaps that might be the pattern for the rest of her life and she was coming to terms with that.

And then out of nowhere, this had happened.

And it had been her idea. Lisa wasn't sure whether it had been a moment of madness, or possibly a moment of sanity. She was only sure that she seemed to be going through with it. And she felt kind of . . . excited.

Chucking her bag into the boot, Lisa slipped into the driver's seat. She slotted her key into the ignition and put her road atlas on the passenger seat. (Satnavs were one of the many modern things Lisa was scared of.) She had carefully plotted the route in black marker pen, each relevant page flagged with a different coloured Post-it note. She took a deep breath. In through the nose, one, two, three. Out through the mouth, one, two three.

She looked at the purple troll that hung from the rear-view mirror. 'Don't think about it, Lisa,' she said aloud. 'Don't think about it, don't think about it, don't think about it.'

Strangers from the Internet.

Of course the moment she tried not to think the thought, it appeared. And it was massive and neon green in colour and flashing like the lights outside a strip club.

'I'm going to meet people from the Internet,' Lisa said to Troll, hearing her own voice, high and tense. '*Strangers from the Internet*. These are people I have only ever known on the Captain Ross Poldark fan forum, poldarlings.com. STRANGERS FROM THE INTERNET. They are the very people who everyone knows *are* most likely to be crazy, perverts and murderers.'

Her breaths started coming in short tight bursts. She clenched the steering wheel so hard she could see the whites of her finger joints.

'I'm going to meet strangers from the Internet. Strangers. From. The. Internet.' The big, scary thought made Lisa feel very, very small, like a bug that could be so easily crushed under foot.

'Don't think about it, Lisa,' Lisa said aloud once more. She turned the engine on and opened her road atlas to the first page of the journey. 'You want to do this. You want to go to Cornwall and find Captain Poldark in real life. It's your dream. The only one you've had since . . . Remember that's why you are doing this, you want to find Captain Poldark. And you'd be far too scared to do it alone. You don't have any friends in real life that would travel over four hundred miles, mostly along B roads, to see a man in a three-cornered hat with a scythe.

'The only people that would come with you are these people, people you've been chatting to almost every day since the first series of *Poldark* was on TV. I mean, yes, technically they are strangers. But they are strangers that you know. So don't think about it, Lisa. Just do it. For once in your life just do it. This is the only way you are going to find Captain Ross Poldark, also known as Aidan Turner, and tell him what he's meant to you. You are not an idiot, Lisa. You know he probably won't even care, but that doesn't matter. All that matters is that you will have done something you've dreamt about doing, something that seemed impossible. And maybe, Lisa, just maybe, if you can do that then . . . well, everything else can seem more manageable too. And you won't have to be so afraid anymore.'

Lisa took the handbrake off, and pulled out of her parking space.

At last she was on the road. The first stop was Dudley where she was going to pick up her first passenger, username: @I_AM_DEMELZA.

Of course it was going to take her much longer to get to Dudley than it would take most people, more than twice as long. But that was the trouble when you were too scared to drive on anything but a B road, it always took a long time to get anywhere.

'It's not the destination,' Lisa said. 'It's the journey.'

And then she remembered Captain Poldark, and his dark and stormy eyes, and thought that in this case, it was the destination. It was totally the destination.

CHAPTER TWO

* *

DEMELZA

Location: 13 Waverly Drive, Dudley
Radio station: Free Radio Black Country
Track playing: 'Hanging on the Telephone' by Blondie
Miles travelled: 153.7
Miles until Captain Poldark: 389.8

Fifteen minutes ticked by as Lisa sat outside 13 Waverly Drive looking at @I_Am_Demelza's house, trying to assess it for risk. It was a nice, neat semi-detached house with bay windows and fresh white net curtains. The garden was nicely done, and when Lisa rolled down the window, the scent of the roses in the front border drifted in through the window. It didn't look like the house of a serial killer, she thought. Then again, what was she expecting, a massive flashing sign reading 'ENTER AT YOUR OWN RISK. I QUITE LIKE CHOPPING PEOPLE UP AND WEARING THEIR HEADS AS HATS'?

'Lisa Murray was the fifth victim of the Head Hat murderer,' Lisa muttered in *Crimewatch* style. 'She had been totally unsuspecting on that bright summer's day as she approached his lair of doom.'

'Here goes nothing,' she told Troll. Troll didn't even blink.

Getting out of the car, she locked it and checked the handle three times. She clutched her car keys in her fist, went up the white painted steps, and rang the doorbell. The first few bars of 'Amazing Grace' sounded.

It was nearly enough for Lisa to turn on her heels, run down the steps, then leap into the car and press central locking. Except that the door opened almost at once, and her mum had brought her up to be much too polite to just run away, even from someone she thought might be criminally insane.

'Hello love, you must be Lisa?' A woman of about seventy smiled at Lisa.

'Demelza?' Lisa asked, because if she was honest she had rather been expecting a pretty young woman with a mass of red curls and stunning figure to open the door. Possibly carrying a chainsaw. But this was cool. She was pretty sure she could take this old lady in a fight.

She followed her into a neat and airy living room. China cats pranced on the mantelpiece and a bronze carriage clock ticked neatly on the sideboard.

'Oh dear me, no,' Not Demelza chuckled. 'No, no, my Demelza days are long over, sad to say. I was a fan the first time round. No, no, it's Ray you've come to pick up, but he's not quite ready yet, I think he's having trouble with his scar.'

Any one of the words in that sentence would ordinarily have sent fear pulsing through Lisa's veins, but all of them at once almost stopped her heart in instant dread. Ray. He. Scar.

'I'm sorry, I've got to go,' Lisa said.

Get out, get out, get out, get out, was all she could think, scrambling for the front door. Danger, danger, danger!

'Lisa, dear!' Not Demelza called out. 'Please, wait. You don't understand. Ray, he needs this. Please don't go!'

Lisa stopped at the front door, flung it open, and stepped outside onto a welcome mat that read 'Home Sweet Home'. In that place of relative safety she felt a little calmer. After all she could always gouge out an eye with her car keys before making a dash for the car, pressing central locking and calling the police. She turned around to face Not Demelza.

'The thing is I didn't know that @I_Am_Demelza was a man,' she explained. 'He never said. Which is classic creep behaviour. And I don't really feel able to drive several hundred miles with a man that I don't know. You can see where I am coming from, right? Unless you and him have the whole Norman Bates thing going on.'

'Norman who?' Not Demelza's face crumpled into a picture of sadness, and instantly Lisa felt sorry.

'You're right. Of course you are,' Not Demelza said. 'Ray should have told you who he was. I told him. "Ray," I said, "you need to tell them you're a fella. They aren't going to like finding out at this stage." But he thought that, if you found out before today, you would have uninvited him.'

'Well, he was right,' Lisa said.

'The thing is he's really been looking forward to this trip. He really needs this. He's been so down since he got out of the army, and he hasn't got many friends . . .'

'So you're telling me he's an ex-army loner who lives with his mum?' Lisa said. 'You're not exactly selling him.'

'But if you think about it,' Not Demelza replied, 'who better to protect you on your journey than a soldier?'

'We're going to Bodmin, not Mordor,' Lisa said. Although, in truth, to her both destinations seemed equally scary.

'Lisa, hi, great to meet you . . .' Ray said as he arrived at the bottom of the stairs, wearing a frock coat and knee-length leather boots.

Lisa decided not to try to eye gouge. Instead she raced straight for the safety of her Micra and locked all the doors. She'd already dialled 999 when Ray arrived at her window. Her finger hovered over the call button.

Ray crouched down outside. 'Lisa? What's wrong?'

Lisa stared at him through the window.

What's wrong? Lisa thought. You're a man whose fan-forum username is 'I Am Demelza', and who turns out to be six-foot tall. You're also built like a mountain, dressed in full Captain Poldark uniform, complete with a fake scar down one cheek – the wrong cheek, by the way – and you want to know what's wrong?

But she didn't say any of that. She just sat in her car, with the windows rolled up, staring. Maybe if she stayed very still he would just go away. And the police were just a call away – although she couldn't be sure how much of a threat they would see in a Captain Poldark tribute act.

'Lisa, just open the window, just a crack,' Ray said. One of the black curls from his nylon wig trembled in the breeze. 'Hear me out, please?'

Lisa looked at Troll, and Troll stared right back at her.

'Fine,' she said, pressing the button that lowered the window a couple of inches. '*I am Demelza*? I don't bloody think so. Look, I'm sure you've got reasons. We've all got reasons, but this was a bad idea, a stupid idea. I'm going home.'

'I'm sorry.' Ray crouched down and took off his hat, and with it came the wig revealing short reddish-blond hair. 'I know I should have said. I should have made it clear that I was a guy . . .'

Lisa raised an eyebrow. 'Oh you think?'

'But I never said that I *wasn't*. You lot just assumed I was a girl. And after we'd been chatting for weeks, I thought if I bring it up now that's just going to seem even weirder. And I really looked forward to talking to you on Poldarlings. Then you came up with the idea of the trip. I thought, if I mention it now, they definitely won't want me to come, and then I thought . . . I don't know what I thought. I suppose I'd hoped it would just work out in the end.' He shrugged and looked so sad that for a moment Lisa felt sorry for him.

'Why not I_Am_Poldark?' she asked him. 'Why Demelza?'

'I thought you'd be even more freaked out if I turned up dressed as Demelza.' Ray half smiled. 'I've got that costume in my luggage. I do a pretty good accent too.'

Lisa stared hard at him, and then suddenly she saw the truth.

'Oh I see,' she said. 'Yes, I get it. Why didn't you just say?'

'About me being a bloke? Well, because . . .'

'I mean, no one cares anymore if you're gay. Although I suppose maybe in the army it would still be tricky . . .?'

'Um.' Ray took a breath. 'Look, cards on the table. I got out of the army over a year ago. Medical discharge, depression, some other stuff. I haven't had any luck getting a job. When I came out of the army I thought there was someone waiting for me, someone who really loved me.

But I was wrong. I got home and well . . . let's just say they didn't invite me to the wedding.'

'Oh,' Lisa said, then lowered the window another inch or two. She knew something about heartbreak and betrayal. She knew how it could make a person different, make it so they didn't even recognise themselves any more. 'I'm sorry. The person you loved married someone else?'

'Er . . . yes,' Ray said, after a very slight pause. 'That pretty much covers it.'

'Was it very hard, being in the army, being gay?' Lisa asked, thoughtfully.

'Well, I mean, yes, and no,' Ray said, lowering his gaze. 'Lisa, I'm just a sad bloke who lives at home with his mum and has a Demelza wig in his bag. That's the person you've been talking to on Poldarlings all this time. That's me. I've never written anything that isn't true about me, or what I think about the series, or the characters, or actors, or the books. And I thought you and me, we got on pretty well, had a laugh. It will be just the same, over the next few days, I promise. Except we won't need Wi-Fi to talk.'

Lisa opened her window a little more and looked into Ray's brown eyes, which were warm and steady and sweet. Once, Lisa had been able to trust her own instinct about people. Once, she'd been able to look into a person's eyes and decide whether or not to get to know them. That was until she'd got it so completely wrong that she never trusted herself or her instinct ever again.

Was Ray as nice and as kind as his eyes seemed to suggest? She had no idea. What she did know was that she had two options. She could turn around now, go back home and let everyone down, and give up on looking for Captain Poldark. Or she could go all in, and take a chance. At least she was ready for it all to go wrong. That was the one upside of living in a state of constant anxiety – she always had an exit plan.

What's the worst that could happen? Lisa thought, looking at Troll. Apart from becoming a murder victim in a lay-by, that is.

After all she had prepared herself for setbacks like this along the way. She had known from the moment that she'd suggested the trip that there would be times when she would be frightened, and would want to give up and go home. She just hadn't expected one of those times to be so soon, and dressed in a white ruffled shirt.

'So am I going to have to fight you for Captain Poldark then, hey Demelza?' Lisa asked Ray, with a tiny smile.

'Oh there won't be a fight,' Ray said, breaking into a grin. 'He's all mine.'

'Funnily enough, I think our next companion *might* have something to say about that,' Lisa said.

CHAPTER THREE

• •

ABBY

Location: 24 Emmeline Pankhurst Way, Hemel Hempstead

Radio station: Mix 96

Track playing: 'Ghost Town' by The Clash

Miles travelled: 290

Miles until Captain Poldark: 253.5

'It's round here somewhere,' Lisa said, as they circled the block one more time looking for the address @MarryMeAidan78 had given her. 'She said look for Germaine Greer Avenue and turn left at Marie Curie Drive . . .'

'I haven't seen one of these for years,' Ray said, holding the road atlas open on his lap, scratching his neck where the lace collar of his shirt was chafing. 'I didn't think anyone still used them. Not that you even have to use satnavs any more. It's all on your phone these days. The whole world is on your phone these days.'

'Not on my phone, it isn't,' Lisa said, pointing at her 2003 Nokia, which sat in the cup holder between the driver and passenger's seat.

'But . . .' Ray picked it up and stared at it. 'That should be in a museum. How does it even still work?'

'Very well,' Lisa said. 'Calls and texts, that's all I want. I don't want the entire world knowing where I am all the time. I don't want people to be able to find me. I don't want all the crap on the Internet streaming into my pocket. I don't want people to know what I had for lunch or what kind of mood I am in, via a picture of a smiley or frowny face. I don't want the government reading my emails.'

'Yeah, but if you've done nothing wrong you've got nothing to worry about.'

Lisa shook her head. 'That isn't the point at all. What if the people who are looking at all your stuff are the bad guys, out to get you. It's much better to keep your head down, keep a low profile, try not to get noticed. I only use the Internet at home, and I'm not too keen on that. If it wasn't for Poldarlings, I might not use it at all . . .'

'Do you wear a tin foil hat too?' Ray joked, and Lisa shot him a look.

'But seriously what are you worried about? Who do you think is after you?'

'Where do I begin?' Lisa said. 'Fraudsters, thieves, perverts, the government, people who want to . . . Wait! There it is!' She pulled into a small car park, behind a new-looking apartment block. 'This is where @MarryMeAidan78 lives. It looks OK . . . Or at least it doesn't look like a crack house, or organised crime syndicate.'

'Not unless gangsters like their window boxes full of flowers,' Ray said.

Lisa looked at him. 'Let's just hope she is who she says she is, and not a truck driver called Cyril.'

✦

'All right?' @MarryMeAidan78 opened the door and nodded at them, offering a very firm handshake. 'I'm Abby, Abs to my mates.'

Abby looked about thirty. Her blonde hair was tied into a short ponytail, pulled back tightly from her round face. She seemed to be dressed as if she were about to storm an embassy. She wore a black T-shirt and combat trousers tucked into biker boots.

'Hi, I'm Lisa, @CornwallLover. And this . . . well, this is @I_Am_Demelza, who is sort of a bloke. Well, no *sort of* about it. He is one. A man.'

'The fuck?' Abby said, looking hard at Ray. 'Demelza's a dude!'

'Yes, but he's gay,' Lisa said quickly. 'He's called Ray.'

'And Ray is gay, huh?' Abby looked Ray up and down very slowly. 'Shame, you're quite fit for a ginger.'

'He just got out of the army,' Lisa added, as if that somehow explained everything.

'Serve in Afghanistan?' Abby asked him, suddenly standing up a little straighter.

'Yes,' Ray said.

'Still got all your bits?' Abby asked.

'Seem to have,' he said.

'I'm in the army,' Abby told him. 'Territorial Army – TA. Not official TA, more like a club. Not a big club – mostly it's just me – but it's just as good as the TA, if not better. We . . . I . . . go up to the common every third Saturday, practise survival skills, living off worms that sort of thing. You ever lived off a worm?'

'Not recently . . .' Ray said. 'I had a can of beef stew that was four months out of date once.'

'Right.' Abby nodded. 'Well, as long as we are all being honest about ourselves, I think I should tell you I'm schizophrenic. Diagnosed when I was nineteen. Anyway, I'm fine now. When I say fine, I mean I'm still schizophrenic, but I've got a lot of support, meds, a counsellor, friends, some of whom actually exist!'

Ray and Lisa exchanged a look.

'That was a schizophrenia joke,' Abby said. 'The thing is, I know people are scared of mental illness. I know a lot of people think it means violence and danger. So if you guys don't want me to come, then I understand.'

Lisa thought for a moment.

'Well, I spent all of last night sleeping under my bed,' she said. 'I don't think I can tell anyone else what normal is.'

Ray smiled. 'Yeah, what Lisa said.'

'Well, it's good to be on board, Ray,' Abby said, punching him so hard on the arm that he winced.

'I'm ready when you are,' she said, showing them into her neat living room, which was filled with a mountain of luggage. 'I've packed the basics: tent, sleeping bag, gas burner, tins of beans times four, emergency chocolate bars times twenty-four, Chardonnay, two bottles. It's Tesco own brand. I don't drink, but it's for you – and it can double up as an antiseptic in an emergency. Right, Ray?'

'If you say so,' Ray said as Abby hefted one of two backpacks onto her shoulders.

'Thing is,' Lisa said, slowly, 'I only have a small car and we still have to pick up @PoldarkGoals. And although I really admire your planning, I think some of this will have to stay behind. Maybe the tent. I've booked us places to stay already, remember? I sent the links in my email to you all.'

'I don't like to leave the tent,' Abby said, rubbing her chin thoughtfully. 'I always think a tent is key in a "Woman against nature" survival event. Although I suppose we could make a shelter from branches . . .'

'It's just that we booked places to stay . . .' Lisa said again.

Abby shrugged. 'Right then, we'll leave the tent. Adapt, that's the key. Adapt. And anyway, if something goes wrong with the bookings, what's better than sleeping outside with a view of the stars?'

'Almost anything,' Lisa said.

For a few seconds the three of them, Internet friends, stood there in silence, none of them sure what should happen next.

'So then, Team Poldark,' Lisa said at last. 'Let's hit the road, get ready to roll and burn up the highway!'

'Via Reading train station first, though. Yeah?' Abby said, remembering the last pick up.

'Yes, totally via Reading first,' Lisa said.

CHAPTER FOUR

★★★★★★★★★★★★★★★★★★★★★★★★★

KIRSTY

Location: Reading train station

Radio station: BBC Radio Berkshire

Track playing: 'It Must Have Been Love' by Roxette

Miles travelled: 335

Miles until Captain Poldark: 208.5

Lisa pulled into the dropping-off zone and scanned the pavement outside the station. When she left that morning, she hadn't expected any problems with working out who @PoldarkGoals was. Lisa had been told she'd be wearing purple Converse, and wearing her hair in braids. However, that was before Ray, who was not a girl, and Abby, who liked eating worms. The worms worried Lisa more than Abby's mental health issues.

Kirsty had been the last to join the trip, and Lisa had been wary about accepting her. @PoldarkGoals was only rarely on the forum, and when she was, she barely commented at all. You'd just see her there in the background, her cursor blinking.

Lisa, Ray and Abby had discussed the details of the trip in a private Internet group that Lisa had made for them, over a couple of weeks. During that time, Lisa had changed her mind about going through with it, almost every hour. She knew she needed to find Captain Poldark. She knew she needed to see him and look into his eyes, and that when she did, all her fear, all her anxiety, would drain away for a few seconds at least.

It didn't even matter that the man she was looking for wasn't anything like the Captain Poldark in her head. What mattered was what finding him would mean to her. And, even if it was just for those few seconds, it would be worth it. Just to feel half a minute of peace, to know that just once in her life she hadn't been afraid.

Then right at the last minute @PoldarkGoals said she suddenly had some time off work, and could she please come too? She said she had money, and a credit card, and there was just something, something in between the words she typed on the forum that seemed so . . . full of need. And Lisa wasn't about to turn down someone for that. She'd welcomed @PoldarkGoals to their trip. She'd loosely arranged a time to meet and had told her the colour and make of her car.

There were several young women, and a couple of lads hanging about outside the ticket office. Two girls were part of a group and one was on her own, standing by a rubbish bin, her shoulders hunched, her chin down. She was tall and slender, and she was carrying a small floral rucksack. She clutched the straps tightly, her pretty face narrow, pale and pinched. There was no purple Converse in sight, and yet there was something about her.

Lisa watched as the girl scanned the cars that came and went, before focusing on Lisa's Micra. Glancing over her shoulder, she ran towards the car, opened the back door and jumped in.

'Whoa there,' Abby said, as the girl slid in next to her. 'You shouldn't surprise me like that. I'm a yellow belt. Anything could happen.'

'Sorry,' the girl said. 'I'm Poldark Goals. My real name's Kirsty? I'm sorry I'm not wearing the trainers. I was at work, and I forgot them and I ran out of time to go home, so . . . who's he?'

Lisa twisted round in her seat and looked at Kirsty. She'd said on the forum that she was twenty-one but she looked much younger.

'He's @I_Am_Demelza,' she said before Ray could answer. 'But it's OK, he's gay.'

'Right,' Kirsty said. 'So he's OK?'

'I think so,' Lisa said.

'Seriously,' Ray said. 'Not all men are evil, you know. I'm a Poldark fan, just like you.'

'And anyway,' Abby said, smiling at Kirsty, 'if he turns out to be a dickhead, I'll break both his legs and we'll leave him in a hedge.'

'OK,' Kirsty said. 'Seems fair.'

'Are you OK?' Lisa asked. 'You look . . . well, a bit stressed out.'

'Fine, fine. I rushed here, after work, and forgot a few things. I was worried I might miss you, or you'd go without me because of the trainers. Should we get going?'

Lisa smiled, wanting to reassure the younger woman. 'Well, you're here now. And we're all set. We'd better get on the road if we want to make our B&B before dark.'

CHAPTER FIVE

★★★★★★★★★★★★★★★★★★★★★★★

Location: Restful Haven Bed and Breakfast
Radio station: BBC Radio 2
Track playing: 'Knowing Me, Knowing You' by Abba
Miles travelled: 350.3
Miles until Captain Poldark: 193.2

'All I'm saying,' Ray said, 'is that Restful Haven sounds a
bit like a funeral parlour.'

'No, it does not,' Lisa said, as she peered out of her
windscreen at the guest house. Its walls were black against
the darkening sky. 'Restful is a nice word. Haven is a nice
word. There is nothing deathly about either. That's why I
chose it! If it was something to do with funerals, it would
be Green Meadows, or Heaven's Gate or . . .'

'Restful Haven,' Abby said, unhelpfully from the
back seat.

'Well, it isn't,' Lisa said with more confidence than
she felt. The spiky outline of the house did look a little
creepy against the moonlit sky. 'And it beats sleeping in
the car.'

'You OK?' Lisa asked Kirsty, the last to get out. She looked tired, as if she hadn't had a good night's sleep in a very long time. There was something else about her too, that Lisa couldn't quite define. But whatever it was it troubled her. It didn't frighten her exactly, which would had been normal, for Lisa anyway. No, instead for some reason Lisa felt protective of Kirsty, frightened *for* her. And then she realised why.

Kirsty reminded her of herself, the way she'd been after her mum died and everything went wrong. And that surprised Lisa. She'd thought for a long time that she'd been stuck in that moment, ever since. But that wasn't true. She didn't have the same look that Kirsty had any more. And yes, her journey from there to here had been long, twisted and mostly in the wrong direction, but still she'd got this far. Which meant that maybe, just maybe, she could get even better. She could even perhaps become the person she had once been.

As soon as Lisa had that thought it terrified her. That person had been the reason she'd got into this state in the first place. Being that person again simply wasn't an option. Keep your head down, stay invisible, and keep an eye on Kirsty, Lisa thought. That you can do.

Kirsty smiled feebly. 'I'm fine.' It was the most she'd said since she got into the car. She'd sat silently in the corner listening to Ray and Abby argue over the best way to skin a rabbit. And after that Abby had told them an unlikely story. She had once got all the way to Gary Barlow's dressing-room door, she said, and had rung the bell before security threw her out.

'It is a bit weird, isn't it?' Lisa said, trying to get Kirsty to talk. 'Going on holiday with a bunch of strangers.'

'A bit.' Kirsty shrugged. 'But it's not as bad as it is at the home.'

'The home?'

Kirsty shrugged again. 'Home, just home. It's just . . . I just broke up with my boyfriend, that's all.'

'Oh I see. I'm sorry.' That made sense to Lisa. When you were Kirsty's age, boyfriends seemed like the most important things in the world, the be-all and end-all.

Of course, what with not going out, not using social media, and barely using the Internet, she hadn't had a boyfriend of her own since . . . well, since the last one, which was almost six years ago now.

But honestly, Lisa didn't care. She didn't need a real man in her life, not when she had someone a thousand times better than reality could ever create. She had Captain Ross Poldark to wrap her in his manly arms and throw her wantonly onto a four-poster bed and rip off her top any time she wanted. In her head anyway.

'Are you two going to stand there gabbing all night?' Abby called from the doorway of the B&B where a lone bulb flickered over the entrance.

'Coming!' Lisa called back, hooking her arm through Kirsty's. 'Try and put it out of your mind. Just think this time tomorrow we'll be halfway to Captain Poldark!'

'Yay,' Kirsty cheered, but somehow her heart didn't seem in it.

✻

'Two twin rooms, yes?' Mrs March, the landlady, said. She yawned to show them exactly how late it was. It was only just after nine, but apparently at Restful Haven guests who hadn't checked in by seven were frowned upon. She slid two keys with large numbered tags across what wasn't so much a reception desk as a reception coffee table.

'Oh! That was before we found out Demelza was a man!' Lisa said, biting her lip.

'I beg your pardon?' Mrs March, narrowed her eyes. 'All bookings are non-refundable.'

'Yes, I see. It's just that . . .' She turned around and looked at Ray. 'Well, our party changed at the last minute and I'm not sure that any of us feel comfortable about sharing with a gentleman. Do you have any other rooms?'

'Fully booked,' Mrs March said, darkly. 'Only got three rooms. You've got two and I'm keeping my husband in the other until he sees the error of his ways.'

'Oh.' Lisa turned to Abby who didn't seem nearly as bothered by the frightening Mrs March as *she* was.

'No worries, I can sleep in the car,' Ray said.

'Or I can,' Abby said. 'I can sleep anywhere. I once slept standing up inside a hollow tree. Best night's sleep I ever had.'

Lisa thought about handing over the keys to her little car to someone she'd only really known for a few hours and clasped them tighter in her fist.

'No . . . No, it's OK. I'm sure we could work it out. Though I think Kirsty should share with one of us. What do you think?' she asked Abby.

'Well, he's not likely to ravage us in our sleep, is he?' Abby said. 'And even if he is, one simple chop to the throat, quick double-eye jab, and I'd fell him like a tree.'

'Can you decide?' Mrs March said, looking at her watch. 'Some of us would like to go to bed before dawn.'

'Toss you for him,' Abby said, fishing a fifty-pence piece from her combat trousers.

Lisa lost the toss.

*

'Why Poldark?' Ray's voice cut into the dark, just as Lisa was about to drift off to sleep. Of all the things she had expected from sharing the tiny twin room with a virtual stranger with a penis, she hadn't expected it to be so . . . well, so easy.

They'd barely spoken a word to each other since they'd shut the bedroom door. Ray had waited politely on his bed while Lisa had changed into her PJs in the small bathroom.

Then Lisa had got into her bed and pulled the covers up to her chin as she'd listened to Ray clean his teeth.

When he'd eventually emerged, wearing jogging bottoms and a T-shirt, he'd gotten into bed and they'd turned out the light. Lisa had lain in the dark marvelling at herself.

If anyone had said to her that tonight she'd be sharing a room with a strange man and actually feeling pretty OK about it, she'd have laughed in their faces. But here she was, being crazy, carefree and playing with fate, and she liked it.

Closing her eyes she imagined herself in a crowded ballroom as Ross Poldark swept in, glowering at everyone there, until his gaze fell on her. Unable to tear his eyes away from her, he moved towards her, took her into his arms and . . .

'Why Poldark,' Ray asked again. 'I mean why does it mean so much to you?'

Lisa thought for a moment. She wasn't exactly sure how to explain it.

'Escape,' she said after a while. 'For a long time I've been . . . sort of trapped, I suppose. In my house, in my job – I'm a school librarian. In my life, in my head. Afraid. Books open doors and windows for me. They let me look out at the world. Then I started to read the Poldark books when the TV series came back on, and . . . well, to be honest I fell in love. With the places and the characters and the stories. But most of all, most of all I fell in love with Ross. He's so strong and brave. He's not perfect. I know that. He's moody, impetuous, hot-blooded . . .'

'Not real . . .' Ray said sleepily.

'I know, I know he's not real.' Lisa smiled in the dark. 'But . . . I don't know how to explain it, except that I think that's part of the reason I love him. A book boyfriend can do everything to make you happy, and nothing to hurt you. If a book boyfriend looks like he's going to be trouble, all you have to do is shut the pages, and then they can't get out. They can't come after you. And when I think about Ross – and his hat, and his horse – I feel safe. I suppose that sounds kind of crazy, doesn't it? Ray?'

A gentle snore came from under Ray's covers, and Lisa smiled to herself. She rolled over onto her side, turning her back on him. If she pretended very hard, she could imagine that the roar of Ray's snores was the crash of the waves against the wild Cornish coastline.

Now Captain Poldark, she thought, where were we?

CHAPTER SIX

* *

Location: On the road (B3139)
Radio station: Radio Now FM
Track playing: 'I Want to Break Free' by Queen
Miles travelled: 393.3
Miles until Captain Poldark: 150.2

The Micra cruised down the B3139 taking the long way round, via Glastonbury. The sun broke through the clouds and turned the tarmac to silver. Lisa put down the window an inch or two.

'What are you going to say when you meet him?' Abby asked Lisa. 'My future stud-muffin/ husband man-meal . . . Aidan, I mean.'

'I don't know,' Lisa replied. 'It's complicated.'

'Complicated!' Abby laughed. 'It's not that complicated. I'm going to get him to sign my boobs. With his tongue. What about you, Kirsty?'

'I don't know.' Kirsty turned towards the window. 'I'm not really into the whole groupie thing.'

'Groupie thing!' Lisa laughed. 'I'm not a groupie. I'm a . . . fan. I'm a Poldarling. And that's why it's complicated. I mean, on the one hand, we're off to where they are shooting the next series. We want to see them filming. We want to meet the cast. But it's not really Aidan Turner that I want to meet . . .'

'Although she wouldn't kick him out of bed for eating biscuits! Hey, Ray, hey?' Abby leaned forward and patted Ray on the shoulder.

Ray laughed so heartily that he made the Troll quiver.

For some reason he had kept his seat next to her. None of them had moved from their places on day one, and Lisa had to admit she liked that. It beat the inflatable man she kept in the glove box for the evenings when she came home late from work and didn't want people to think she was driving alone. Especially since her inflatable man had got that puncture which made his head a bit floppy.

'Well, anyway,' Lisa said, 'as nice as Aidan is, it's not him that I love. It's Ross. It's Ross whose eyes I want to look into, whose hands I want to grip me so hard I . . .'

'Whoa, hold on now,' Ray said. 'I mean you realise that's not going to happen, don't you? If we are lucky enough to meet any of the cast . . . well, they're real people, not characters. All I'm saying is that you don't want to get yourself a restraining order as a souvenir.'

'I had one of those once,' Abby muttered. 'Daniel Craig gave it to me. Got it framed.'

'Well, that's rich coming from six-foot Demelza,' Lisa said. 'Why are you on this trip, Ray? What's in it for you? Why do you like Poldark so much?'

Ray didn't answer for a moment. He dipped his chin as he lifted a buttock and searched for a stick of chewing gum in his back pocket.

'I suppose it's not Captain Poldark I'm searching for,' he said. 'I suppose it's me.'

'You?' Abby leaned forward. 'What you talking about, soldier?'

'Look, I know you've got that hat and everything, but you do see that that's role play, right?' Lisa joked.

Ray rolled his eyes. 'Obviously. What I mean is, I do relate to him. I mean me and Poldark . . . we both went to war, fighting for a cause that we didn't really understand. We came back and we weren't the same. The people we thought would always be there for us, they'd moved on. Left us behind. Ross Poldark, he finds a place for himself again, a reason to go on. He thinks he's never going to feel anything. for anyone. Or do anything important again. But he does. He found himself, love and a sense of purpose on the cliffs of Cornwall. So . . . if *he* can, then maybe I can too. Because, I don't know, I just don't think I'm going to find myself in Dudley.'

'Oh my god, the Little Chef that time forgot!' Abby said, pointing out of the window. 'Pull over, Lisa. I'm starving. Ray might want to find himself in Cornwall, but I want to find myself tits-deep in an all-day full English.'

★

'I liked what you said, before,' Lisa said to Ray over a milky coffee. Abby had gone out for a fag, and Kirsty had been in the Ladies for a very long time. 'About coming on this trip to find yourself. I'm sorry I got a bit snappy. It means something to you, and I like that.'

'Do you?' Ray said. 'I like you too.'

Lisa poured another sachet of Sweet'N Low into her coffee. That wasn't exactly what she had said, or what she had meant. It was nice that Ray was so friendly. But it was confusing too.

She had purposely kept men out of her life ever since Him, and now . . . well, of course Ray didn't like her *that* way. After Him she wasn't sure if she wanted any man, any real man, to like her *that* way again. But even with Ray, even with a bloke who would only ever be her friend, she was unsure.

Hanging around with people was nice. It was fun. She'd laughed more in the last day and a half than she had in a very long time. But what if she let these people into her life, and called them her friends? What if something terrible happened again? What if when you really needed the people you thought you could count on, they weren't there?

Lisa didn't think she could go through that again.

'I think you'll do it,' she said to Ray. 'Find yourself. Or at least find another beginning, anyway.'

'You're a lovely person, Lisa.' Ray smiled.

Lisa felt a tiny thrill start somewhere at the base of her spine, and tingle up towards her neck. Suddenly her heart was thumping . . . not from excitement but fear. Standing up suddenly, she knocked over Kirsty's glass of flat Coke, which ran off the table top and right into Ray's lap.

'I just need to . . .' Lisa pointed towards the Ladies, hurrying away before Ray could see that her hands were shaking.

What had he done? What had he said that had frightened her so much? Lisa knew the answer of course. She knew it, but she didn't want to admit it. He'd smiled at her, and it reminded her of Frank. Of the way Frank used to smile at her – like she was the only woman in the world. And now she was shaking and she wanted to go home. She wanted to bolt and triple-lock the door, shut all the curtains, climb into bed with a book and just forget the world.

But Lisa was very far from home.

Pushing her way into the Ladies, she rushed into a cubicle and locked the door. It would be tricky, she thought frantically. But if she could wait until all three of them were busy, paying the bill or something, she could sneak out of the fire door. Then she could leave their stuff in the car park and just go home.

She could just drive to the next roundabout, make a U-turn and go home. Go back to her little flat, and her little job, and her little life and stay there, where she would be safe. Safe from harm, safe from smiles and laughter. There wasn't an option. There wasn't another way to stop this fear that had come up from her toes, and was gripping hold of her heart so hard that it hurt. The only thing that would work would be to go home.

'Lisa?' Kirsty's voice, whisper-thin and full of tears, came from the cubicle next door. For a moment Lisa wondered about not answering. But she could see Kirsty's feet under the cubicle wall. Which meant that Kirsty could probably see hers.

'Yes?' Lisa replied, hoping that Kirsty didn't notice the tremble in her voice. She just had to wait for Kirsty to leave and then, as soon as she had, she could still make her planned getaway.

'Can I . . . can I tell you something?' Kirsty asked, her voice echoing off the tiles.

'Do you want me to come out?' Lisa asked.

'No, just stay there. It's easier to say if I don't have to look at you.'

'What is it?' Lisa frowned. For a moment her own sense of fear faded. 'What's easier?'

'I'm really sorry – I really am – but I lied,' Kirsty said. 'And the thing is, I'm in a terrible mess and I don't know what to do. And I don't want to get you into trouble too, but I don't know what to do . . .'

'Lied about what?' Lisa asked her.

'About being @PoldarkGoals,' Kirsty said. 'I'm not her. Well, I am, sort of. But it's Donna who is the Poldark fan. She's the one who is crazy about Poldark. She'd be on the forum a lot, and sometimes she'd leave her laptop around. I was trying to find a way out. I had a bit of money saved and I was going to see how far I could get on a train with it, while she wasn't looking. And that's when I saw the Poldarlings forum, and you were posting about the trip . . . I set up my own profile and hoped you'd let me come with you. I know it's wrong but I was so scared, and I just couldn't think what to do.'

'Wait a minute, who's this Donna?' Lisa was struggling to keep up with the sudden flow of information.

'She works at the place where I live,' Kirsty told her. 'I live in a care home.'

'A care home?' Lisa turned to face the chipboard wall that separated her from Kirsty. 'That's where you work, you mean?'

'No,' Kirsty said, and Lisa's heart sank. 'No, that's where I live. Lived, until I ran away, with you guys. And the thing is . . . I'm not . . . I'm fourteen.'

'Bloody hell!' Lisa unlocked her door and walked out. 'Bloody hell, Kirsty! You realise what this means, don't you? This means we've accidentally abducted you!'

After a second, Kirsty opened the door and stepped out. As soon as Lisa saw her she knew exactly what the poor girl was feeling. Kirsty looked so afraid, so lost, that all the anger and anxiety that Lisa had felt one moment before melted away.

'Come here,' Lisa said, opening her arms to the girl. 'You look like you need a hug.'

After a moment Kirsty walked into her embrace. Although the girl's arms stayed by her side, Lisa felt Kirsty's muscles relax a little, and her breathing became slow and steady.

'I'll help you,' Lisa said. Thoughts of her own escape were already fading away. 'But you have to tell us – all of us – what it is that you are running away from. The last thing this trip needs is any more lies.'

✻

Another round of milky coffees and another glass of flat Coke. And this time some doughnuts, which nobody touched once Lisa explained what Kirsty had told her.

'Fuck!' Abby said. 'This is serious shit. This is black ops, deep-cover shit. We need to get some wigs.'

'I don't think you're exactly understanding the problem here,' Ray said. He poured another sachet of sugar into his untouched coffee – and that made four, Lisa noticed. 'We three adults have a missing minor in our car with us, who hadn't even met us the day before yesterday. That looks bad, and could get us into serious trouble.'

'Except for one thing,' Lisa said. 'We aren't scumbag evil bastards. We're the good guys, aren't we?'

'Straight-up heroes,' Abby agreed. 'We're like the A-Team in a hatchback.'

'It's the bad guys and the people who have let her down that she's running away from,' Lisa went on. 'And she needs our help. Kirsty, tell them. Tell them what you told me.'

Kirsty looked away. She gazed out of the window at the quiet road and its high hedge. Her light eyes were focusing on something only she could see.

'I met this guy, Charlie,' she said eventually. 'Or, more like he met me. He'd always be there, round the shopping centre after school. I thought he was cool. He had stuff . . . a car, phone, nice clothes. He knew some of my friends, some of the older girls from the home. They all wanted him to look at them. But he kept looking at me. It felt . . . nice.' Kirsty shook her head. 'I know how it sounds.'

'It doesn't sound like anything,' Lisa said.

'When you're in care, you get so used to people looking past you, like you're nothing,' Kirsty said. 'When he looked at me I felt . . . happy, I suppose. He was older, a lot older, but he didn't act it. He made me laugh, told me I was pretty. He'd buy me things, little things, but nice. Things just for myself. He'd take me on dates and treated me nice. At first it was perfect, like you see in movies. Romantic.

'He told me he loved me and he wanted me to show him I loved him . . . so I did. But then he changed after that. He wasn't sweet any more, or kind. He was always angry, and I was always letting him down. He said, if I wanted him to be happy again, for things to be like they were before, then I had to do something for him and his friends.' Kirsty kept turning her glass of Coke round and round between her palms. 'And I knew what it was he wanted me to do. He was arranging this party, and . . . I had to get out, I had to.'

'Christ, Kirsty I'm so sorry.' Ray dropped his head into his hands.

Abby reached a hand across the table, stopping just short of Kirsty's. 'Bastard,' she said, gently. 'Well, he can't get you now. You're safe now.'

'That's the point though,' Lisa said. 'She's not, not in the eyes of the law. She's in a car with three strange adults she met on the Internet. STRANGERS FROM THE INTERNET. I mean we know we're not evil, but police and social services don't. And they'll be looking for her.'

'Kirsty, we have to take you to a police station,' Ray said. 'I know that's not what you want to hear, but it's the only option.'

'When I told him I wouldn't do it, that I'd tell, Charlie said if I ever tried telling someone, they'd just say I was making it up. He said that no one would believe me. Especially not after . . . well, I thought he was my boyfriend,' Kirsty said. 'They'll say it's my fault. No one cares about people like me.'

'We care,' Lisa said, looking at Ray. 'And we'll make other people care. Kirsty, what else can we do except get you legal help?'

'There's a reason I wanted to get to Cornwall,' Kirsty said. 'As soon as I saw where you were all going, I thought it was like a sign or something. When I was little – before Mum got so into drugs, and went to prison – she said my dad had a half-sister down there, in Bodmin, where you're going.

'Mum was always going on about how we'd go there on holiday one summer, although we never did. She was always chasing money, chasing the next hit. It was when she got into dealing that things really got bad. That's when she got sent down.'

Kirsty paused for a moment, as if she was letting everything that had happened in her short life catch up with her. 'Mum said my auntie's name was Alison. I thought I could find her. I thought maybe she might let me stay with her. Bodmin can't be that big, can it? If I ask around. For an Alison who had a half-brother called Pete? I know she works in a café, or at least she did. Please, I don't know what else to do. If Charlie catches me . . . I really think he might kill me.'

Lisa stared into Kirsty's pale-grey eyes, and she realised that, if she was honest, she didn't know what to do either.

'What would Captain Poldark do?' Lisa asked, and Ray looked up at her. She half expected him to laugh, but he didn't.

'He'd do the right thing,' he said. 'He'd protect the weak, even if it meant breaking the law.'

'He'd get her to a place of safety, no matter what it cost him,' Abby said. 'And Demelza would help him.'

'That's right,' Lisa said. 'So we'll do what Poldark would do. We'll get her to Cornwall, to Bodmin – see if we can find this aunt of hers. We'll do what Poldark would do. But look, Ray, Abby – if you want to quit now, then no one would blame you.'

'Are you kidding?' Abby said. 'I haven't had this much fun since I camped out in Olly Murs's back garden. You know, if he'd only let me make him my baked beans special, I think we could have really bonded.'

'OK,' Ray said, 'I'm in. It's been a long time since I felt like I was doing something worthwhile.'

'Thank you,' Kirsty said. 'Thank you so much, but there's something I think I've got to tell you all . . .'

'Something else?' Lisa asked her. 'What?'

'I don't even really like Poldark,' Kirsty said.

CHAPTER SEVEN

****

Location: Black Valley Camp and Caravan Site
Radio station: no reception
Track playing: none
Miles travelled: 427.8
Miles until Captain Poldark: 115.7

'If you let me drive, we could be there tonight,' Ray said to Lisa after they pulled into the campsite. Abby had taken Kirsty to the site office to pick up the keys to their caravan, which Lisa had booked in advance.

The afternoon had grown grey and cold, but that didn't spoil the beauty of the view of the deep Devonshire countryside. Soft hills rolled into one another in one long embrace. Lisa leant against her Micra, breathing in the sense of space all around her. It had been a very long time since she had been this far out in the world . . . a long time since she felt like she could stretch out her arms without touching her own four walls. It was a good feeling.

'The longer we've got her with us, the more likely it is that all of us are going to get into really serious trouble,' Ray added. 'I'm not backing out. I'm just saying. We all have to be aware of that. If you let me drive, we can get her the help she needs sooner.'

'I can't,' Lisa said, tearing her eyes away from the view to look at him. She was still clutching her car keys. 'I'm sorry.'

'But why not?' Ray asked her. 'I'm not a "stranger from the Internet" anymore, am I? We know each other, you and me. You can tell that I'm an all right bloke, can't you? Plus, I used to drive a tank. I'm pretty sure I can handle a hatchback. And the sooner we get to Bodmin tomorrow, the sooner we can try and find her aunt, and get her safe.'

'No, you don't get it,' Lisa said. 'I can't let you drive my car, because . . . it's my exit plan. My escape route. It's my place where I can feel safe wherever I am. I need to know that it's there for me. All the time. I can't let you have the keys. I can't let anyone have the keys. It's like my four-wheeled, portable bomb shelter.'

Lisa looked down. A deep frown made a crease between her eyebrows. 'I *know* how I sound. I *know* I sound crazy. When something really bad happens to you – something so bad that nothing you thought you knew seems right anymore – well, then, you do what you have to do to . . .'

'Try and feel safe,' Ray finished her sentence for her.

Lisa looked up at him. 'You know what I'm talking about?'

Ray smiled. 'Why do you think I'm living at my mum's house, dressing up in costumes?'

Lisa returned the smile. 'Because you're a Poldark geek?'

'Partly that, but partly because . . . when I was in the army I got used to living with constant danger. The next step you take might end in the click of a landmine. Or the next corner you turn might lead you into an ambush. Or that sweet-looking kid with the big eyes who looks so scared might actually try to kill you.

'You live with it, every day. All the time. It gets under your skin like grime, only you can't ever wash it away. And when you come home, you try to go back to a normal life, to being a normal person. But you are still waiting for the click of the landmine. You are still waiting for that kid to throw a grenade. You still feel like every single moment is full of danger.

'I tried living on my own for a bit, but I wasn't ready. So I went home to my mum, aged thirty-seven and six-foot-two-inches tall.' He shook his head, crossing his arms over his chest. 'And I feel like a proper failure.'

'You shouldn't.' Lisa reached out and touched his arm. 'It's not a failure to need your family. I still miss talking to my mum. Six years on and I still think of things I want to tell her.'

'Mum welcomed me back with open arms,' Ray said. 'She always did love sorting me out. And then we started watching Poldark together on a Sunday night, and I really got into it. Joined the Poldarlings. Let everyone think I was a girl. Went on a road trip with a bunch of strangers. And now seem to be slightly on the run.' He laughed, running his palms over his short hair. 'But you know what? And this is really weird. It's gone.'

'What's gone?' Lisa asked.

'That constant feeling of danger. It's gone. When I'm with you, Lisa, I don't feel it. You make me feel brave.'

Just at that moment there was a slight break in the low, dense cloud, and a beam of golden sun lit up the tops of the hills, setting them on fire, like beacons.

'Well, I suppose I feel a bit more like my old self around you lot, too,' Lisa said, looking down, because the way Ray was looking at her was confusing.

'Lisa there's something I . . .'

'Bagsy I get the actual bedroom,' Abby said, as she arrived back jangling keys from her fingers. 'You lot can have the horrible benches.' Abby unlocked the caravan door and all but threw herself inside, causing it to rock and tilt slightly.

'Don't you think Kirsty should get the bedroom?' Lisa said. She doesn't want to be sharing with us lot.'

'I don't mind,' Kirsty said. 'Really. Actually I prefer not to be alone.'

'Well, in that case, Ray gets the bedroom,' Lisa said. 'We can have a girls' sleepover. It will be fun.'

Abby sighed. 'Fine. Anyway, I was thinking. What I could do is go down to those woods over there, catch a few rabbits, gut 'em, skin 'em, and cook 'em up for tea. What do you reckon?'

'*Or*,' Lisa said, 'there *was* that fish and chip shop just a little way back down the road.'

'Fish and chips,' Ray and Kirsty said together.

'This reminds me of holidays when I was a kid,' Abby said.

They'd spent a happy half an hour eating chips from the paper in friendly silence, and she was the first to speak.

'Every summer,' she went on, 'rain or shine. Mostly rain. Me, mum, dad and my three brothers. Six of us in a caravan built for four. Bloody hell, we used to argue, and kick the crap out of each other.' She smiled fondly. 'Good times, good times.'

'Are you close to your family now?' Lisa asked.

Abby looked away for a moment. 'Not really. They never really got me, you know. After I started to have a bit of trouble with the old noggin.' She tapped her forehead. 'I lost it when I was a teenager, really bad. Got sectioned and everything. It was . . . a dark time.

'I think I scared Mum, and we sort of lost touch after that. Even after I was diagnosed, and I started treatment, she never really wanted to hear from me. She always seemed to be out if I called. I'm pretty OK now, really. But I don't think they see *me* any more, not that little kid who used to play Scrabble in a caravan. I think they just see the illness, even though most of the time I'm the sanest person I know.'

She shrugged and smiled. 'But I still see my youngest brother, Eddie. I see him a couple of times a month. Never really liked the other two anyway. They were always dickheads, even as kids.'

Lisa laughed. 'Fine lot we are, aren't we? When I think about it, we are exactly who they are talking about when they say don't meet strangers from the Internet.'

'Except we're not strangers any more, are we?' Ray said. 'To *friends* from the Internet!' He lifted his can of beer and the others returned the gesture, with their glasses and Coke cans.

FRIENDS.

The word glowed soft and golden when Ray said it out loud, and Lisa felt it warm her from the inside out. She had friends again, and she'd had no idea how much that mattered to her until that moment.

'So tomorrow we get to Cornwall, to Bodmin,' Lisa said. 'The chatter on Poldarlings says they'll be filming on the moor all this week. So, first things first. We try to find this café that Alison works in, and then . . . well then, we look for Captain Poldark!'

'We snog the face off Aidan Turner, hey Ray?' said Abby rubbing her hands together. 'I reckon that once I've explained to him how he and I are meant to be together he will totally get it. That's what I reckon. I just need to get him alone. Maybe in a locked room. Maybe with some gaffer tape . . .'

'Abby,' Lisa said sternly. 'You can't abduct Aidan Turner. You can ask him for an autograph – maybe even a photo or a peck on the cheek – but then you have to step away. Got it?'

'Right, yes, got it,' Abby said, winking at Kirsty as if she very much had not got it.

'And if we see him – if we see them – what then?' Lisa asked. 'I mean we've come all this way. But none of us have really thought about what's next after that, have we?'

'A massive disco party,' Abby said, 'with slow dances at the end for smooching.'

'I don't know,' Ray said, 'but I hope, when this is done we will all feel like we've changed, somehow. Moved on a bit. And I really hope we all keep in touch.'

'After I've married Aidan, and it's been covered in *Hello* magazine, we'll have you over to lunch,' Abby said. 'We won't let fame change us.'

'Girls,' Ray said, pushing the last of his chips away from him, 'I need to say something. We've all been sharing stories, and telling the truth about ourselves, being really honest. That's meant a lot to me. I have to tell you all something.'

'You're not a girl, we know.' Abby grinned. 'Or wait! You *are* a girl?'

'I'm not gay,' Ray said simply. 'To be fair, I never said I was. Lisa just assumed . . .'

Abby raised an eyebrow and looked at Lisa.

'What do you mean?' Lisa asked, her tone tense. 'Are you saying you lied to me . . . us . . . *again*?'

'No,' Ray said. 'I never said I was gay. You just thought it, and I felt a bit awkward about correcting you . . . I wanted to come on this trip. I really wanted to come, and I knew you'd feel happier with me being gay . . . so . . .'

'Get out.' Lisa stood up, or at least she tried to, but it was more of a stoop. Her thighs were trapped under the caravan table and her head was bowed by the low ceiling.

'Lisa, come on . . . it's still Ray,' Abby said. 'No harm done.'

'No harm done?' Lisa prised herself out from under the table, climbing over Abby's legs. 'Lots of harm done! You can't ask someone to be your friend – to tell you stuff about themselves and to *trust you* – when you're lying to them the whole time! There is no room for a liar on this trip.'

'Everyone tells lies, now and again!' Abby said. 'So Ray's not gay. So what? That's good news in my book. One less person I have to fight off to get to Aidan.'

'You don't get it,' Lisa said. 'I really thought he was someone I could trust. And you don't know how hard that is for me. I'm going outside and, when I come back, I want him gone.'

'Lisa, please . . .' Ray said. A cold blast of wind snatched his words away and almost knocked Lisa off her feet as she opened the caravan door.

Hugging her arms around her, she ran to her car. She fumbled with her keys in her rush to get in. Once inside, she switched the engine on and pushed the central-locking button. She turned the radio up as loud as it would go, and it filled the car with the noise of static. It had started to rain hard. Drops pelted against the windscreen like handfuls of pebbles.

Breathe in, she told herself. Slowly, breathe in. Slowly, breathe out. You are OK. You are safe. You are OK. You are safe. You are OK. You are safe. You are OK. You are safe.

If she repeated the phrases enough times, sometimes she could trick her body into thinking they were true.

A knock on the window made her jump.

Ray, huddled in the freezing rain, peered through the window. Lisa turned away from him. But he only went round to the other side, looking colder and wetter with every second.

He didn't look like a liar, Lisa thought. If anything he had a nice face. She had come to really like looking at him over the last couple of days. But that was the trouble. Those were the worst kind. The kind that made you believe in them.

Still, no matter what sort of man he was, she didn't want it to be her fault if he became the first man ever to drown in a field.

She turned down the radio and put the window down a little.

'Please let me in,' Ray said. 'Let's talk about it.'

Lisa didn't move.

'Look, Lisa, I don't know what happened to you before, but whatever it was, I'm not going to do the same thing. I'm not. How can I? I'm just a bloke who lives with his mum. I'm a loser with a dead-end job, not much money and no prospects. I'm about as dangerous as a pyjama case! And anyway, you've got Abby looking out for you. I'm more scared of her than I ever was of the Taliban.'

At that Lisa almost smiled, but only almost. She released the central-locking button, nodded at the passenger door and waited.

When Ray got in he was shivering with the cold. 'Typical British summer,' he said.

'I was going to get married,' Lisa told him, because she knew she had to get the words out quickly, before they got stuck in her chest again, heavy and painful. 'His name was Frank. I'd never had a boyfriend at school, or college. I'd got to the age of twenty-five and I thought probably I'd never meet anyone special, and I was OK with it. And then my mum died.

'It had been just us two since I was a little girl, and then she was gone.' Lisa paused, feeling the threat of tears thicken her voice. She waited for a moment, staring at the sheets of water that streamed down the windscreen until she was ready to go on.

'There weren't many people at the funeral: some cousins, and this guy who'd known her from the flower shop she worked in. He was one of her regular customers. Frank. He was kind and sweet, a bit older than me. He said my mum had told him all about me. He stayed by my side for the whole of the funeral, not saying anything, or trying anything. He was just there. And knowing he was there made it a little bit better.

'A few days later he called me at work. I guess I must have told him where that was, though at the time I thought Mum must have told him. We went for coffee. He made me laugh so much, at a time when I really thought I might never feel like laughing again. Two weeks later, he told me he was in love with me, and I said I loved him too, because I did. Three months after that he asked me to marry him, and I said yes.

'I think about a month had gone by when he said his business was in trouble and that he needed a loan to get it working again. He said he'd be able to pay it back within six months. But banks weren't lending, and he'd probably have to let the business go. Mum had left me a bit of money, so I said I would lend it to him. There were more loans after that.'

Lisa bowed her head, curling herself over the pain that uncurled in her stomach when she thought about that look on his face, that sweet smile . . . the way he'd made her feel so cared for and loved. 'He left the day before the wedding. I'd chosen what I wanted, and he'd booked it all because he didn't want me to be stressed by anything. That was what he told me. He said, all you need to do is to turn up and marry me. I couldn't believe he'd just left me like that, but I was still sure he'd come back.

'It wasn't until I started to ring round to cancel flowers and the reception that I realised he'd never booked any of it. It took me a couple more days to realise that my bank account and my savings account had both been cleaned out. I went to the police and they tried to be kind, but you could see by the way they looked at me what they really thought. They thought I was a fool. They said these people read the death notices in the papers. They look for someone on their own, someone who has just been left some money. They set out to take everything they can from them.'

Lisa turned to look at Ray, who was listening with his head bowed, unable to look at her. A drop of freezing rain ran down his nose before rolling off and plopping into his lap. But still he didn't move.

'I thought that he loved me. I thought I was worth being loved. Stupid cow. It wasn't just money he stole. He stole much more than that. He stole everything that made me feel like the world was an OK place to live in, everything that made me feel safe and protected. He stole my trust in people, all people. It's like he put me in prison and threw away the key.'

Ray wiped his damp hand on his damp trousers, and slowly reached out and took Lisa's hand in his.

'I'm so sorry, Lisa,' he said, so gently that Lisa almost cried.

'Look, I know you aren't a bad bloke,' she said. 'Or at least I think I do. But I thought that about him too. So you can see, can't you, why . . . I get worried. I worry about letting people into my life. Especially people who could really hurt me. I have to keep myself safe, you see. I have to keep myself safe.'

Ray's hand slowly began to warm up as he held hers. 'Lisa, I've made mistakes, stupid mistakes. But I want you to know that I would never do anything to hurt you. Not ever. And, if I could protect you from hurt, and pain, then I would.'

Lisa closed her eyes, and turned her face away from him.

'Well, you can stay on the trip,' she said, pulling her hand from his. 'But I think you and Abby should probably get a train home. I thought I could do this. I thought maybe I was ready to live back in the world again, but

I was wrong. It's not your fault. It's mine. I let myself get carried away. Tomorrow we go to Bodmin. We find Kirsty's aunt, and we look for where they're filming and then this is all over. We go back to how life was before.'

'What if we don't want to go back to how life was before?' Ray asked her.

'Well, you can do what you like,' Lisa said, opening the car door and undoing her seat belt. 'After tomorrow it's got nothing to do with me.'

CHAPTER EIGHT

* *

Location: Bodmin, Cornwall

Radio station: NBC Radio

Track playing: 'I'm Gonna Be (500 Miles)' by The Proclaimers

Miles travelled: 539.5

Miles until Captain Poldark: 4

The last leg of the journey was mostly silent, except for the radio, which Abby sang along to loudly and in a Scottish accent. Then she remembered that everyone else was really tense and in a bad mood, so she stopped singing.

At least the sun came out, driving away the low layer of cloud to reveal a fresh blue sky dotted with white fluffy clouds. They were the sort of clouds that looked like dancing giraffes or elephants on roller skates, Lisa thought, although she didn't say that out loud.

They pulled into a pay-and-display car park in Bodmin, and Lisa twisted round in her seat to look at Kirsty.

'So your aunt works in a café,' she said. 'Do you know what it's called?'

'Well, I know what it was called years ago,' Kirsty said, looking worried. 'You know this whole idea is just crazy. I don't know her, and she doesn't know me. She didn't come forward when I got taken into care. Why would anything be different now? Maybe we should just go to a police station and get it over with.'

'No,' Lisa said. 'It's worth a shot to try and find your aunt. We've come this far, and you never know.'

'OK. It was called The Yeast of Bodmin,' Kirsty said, 'because it has its own bakery.'

'Right.' Ray took out his fancy phone and Lisa watched as he put the name into the search engine. 'Well, it's still in business, and it's a five-minute walk from here. Whether or not your aunt still works there, we'll have to wait and see.'

'What if she doesn't want anything to do with me?' Kirsty said, suddenly frightened.

'One step at a time, Kirsty,' Lisa said, reaching behind her for Kirsty's hand. 'One step at a time.'

✸

The Yeast of Bodmin was busy. There were older ladies meeting for coffee and cake and a family of tourists in matching macs. Then there were younger people, sitting at benches, sucking milkshakes through straws, taking selfies and giggling.

Lisa noticed that Kirsty shrank away from the confident young teenagers in the café. She stood behind her and Ray as if trying to make herself invisible.

Behind the counter were two women, one about forty, the other about half that. Both wore red headscarves with white polka dots, tied in jaunty top knots.

'Do you recognise either of them?' Lisa asked.

Kirsty shook her head. 'I don't know,' she said. 'I never met Alison.'

Lisa nodded at a table in the back corner, as far away from other customers as possible.

'You lot sit down. I'll order some teas.' She grabbed Ray's arm. 'Look out for her. She's terrified.'

Ray nodded. 'I will.'

'Hey, Lisa,' Abby called. 'Get some scones too. And jam. And clotted cream.'

'Really?' Lisa raised an eyebrow. 'You want a cream tea now?'

'What? We're in Cornwall, dude. When in Rome and all that shit.'

The group of teenagers burst into laughter, and Kirsty sank even deeper into her seat.

When it was finally Lisa's turn to be served, the younger woman took her order.

'Thanks,' said Lisa and handed over her money. 'I just wondered. Do you know of someone called Alison who works here, or used to?'

The young woman froze for a moment, clutching a handful of change in mid-air. 'Who's asking?' she said.

Lisa nodded over at the table. 'The girl I'm with. Her name is Kirsty – she's Alison's niece, Pete's daughter, although I don't think they've ever met. She's been in care and had a very bad time of it. Alison is the only family she knows of. Look, to tell the truth, she's in trouble and she needs help.'

The girl considered Lisa for a moment before glancing over at the table where Kirsty sat with her head bowed.

'Mum!' she called through the beaded curtain into the kitchen. 'Get out here!'

✴

Alison set down a plate piled high with scones and pots of jam and cream in the middle of the table.

'Bloody hell, you look like him,' was the first thing she said to Kirsty.

'Is that a good thing?' Kirsty asked. She couldn't look her aunt in the eye quite yet.

'He was a handsome man,' Alison said. 'If he'd had even half the brains to match his looks . . . you weren't even born when he was killed on his bike. He didn't even know you were on the way. I tried to keep in touch with your mum, afterwards. I really did. But she was hard to keep track of.'

'I know,' Kirsty said.

'Do you want to tell me what's gone on?' Alison asked. 'Last I heard, she'd got a place with a guy. I mean you were about three then. I should have tried harder to stay in touch. I had no idea you were in care. What happened?'

'Mum went to prison, again,' Kirsty said. 'She's actually better when she's in there than when she's out. At least she's more or less clean from drugs, and stays away from dodgy boyfriends. I see her once a month and she's OK. She's better.'

Alison looked firmly into Kirsty's eyes. 'You've been dealing with this on your own. Didn't you think to call me before? When she first went away?'

'I told my case worker about you.' Kirsty shrugged, looking away. 'He said he'd follow it up.'

'The main thing you need to know,' Lisa said, 'is that Kirsty is a runaway. People are looking for her, and they might be looking for us. She was trying to get to you and so we brought her here, but there might be some fallout, some trouble. We don't know. And –' Lisa looked at Kirsty '– well, some bad things have happened to her. Things that she will need a lot of support to deal with.'

Alison nodded. She pressed her lips into a thin line as Lisa and Kirsty told her everything that had been going on.

'You look like him,' she said again to Kirsty after they'd all run out of words and tears. 'Can I . . . can I give you a hug?'

Kirsty nodded, and Alison folded her into her arms.

'Right, we'll take this one step at a time, OK?' Alison said gently. 'Maybe you and your friends would like to come round to mine. We'll call the local bobby, ask him for advice. We'll sort it all, love. I promise you. And you are not alone anymore. You got me and Cass now, and we won't let you go, I promise.'

Kirsty suddenly sat up, her face turning white as she stared out of the window.

'What?' Abby asked her.

'It's him, Charlie. He's here. He's across the road, but how? Oh shit! He put an app on my phone. He said he wanted to know where I was all the time. Oh god, I forgot – he's been following me this whole time.'

She took her phone out of her pocket and dropped it in a glass of water on the next table.

'Right, let's get out of here,' Lisa said. 'Back way?'

'Go through the kitchen. What should I do?' Alison asked.

'Don't mention that you've seen us,' Lisa said. She picked up a menu with the café's phone number on the bottom. 'We'll call you here.'

'You go,' Ray said. 'I'm going to talk to him.'

'Ray, you can't . . .' Lisa said. 'He's dangerous.'

'Just to slow him down a bit,' Ray hissed as Charlie began to cross the road. 'Nothing major. You guys get going. Hurry!'

The three women rushed out through the kitchen into a small courtyard. Cass closed the door behind them. Lisa heard the bolt slide home.

'The car park is really close,' Lisa said. 'I think we can get to it this way. Let's head down there.'

They ran down the narrow passageway towards trees that Lisa thought meant they were close to the car park. Except for their footsteps there was no sound. But the alley ended in a brick wall that was taller than any of them.

'Epic!' Abby said, leaping up and grabbing hold of the top of the wall. With a mighty effort, she pulled herself up and straddled the wall. She held a hand down to Kirsty. Lisa gave Kirsty a push and Kirsty reached the top of the wall. Between them, Kirsty and Abby pulled Lisa up.

'This is the best day ever,' Abby said, as she jumped off the other side of the wall. They were on the edges of the car park, the little lilac Micra in sight. 'All I need now is some kind of belly crawl through mud, and it will be full-on perfect.'

'We made it!' Lisa said, unlocking the car as they ran towards it. 'Come on.'

'Kirsty!' A voice that Lisa didn't recognise, but that Kirsty clearly did, called her name across the car park. Kirsty didn't move, caught in the moment as if she were frozen in time.

'What you doing, Kirsty?' the man said, as he began to stride across the car park. His shirt was torn and a bruise was forming on his cheek.

If he looked like that, then what did Ray look like, Lisa wondered, and where was he?

'You've had your fun. You've got the attention you've been seeking. But now it's time to go home, babe. Come back to me, where you belong. Don't I always take care of you? Treat you nice. Who are this lot? Do you think a couple of biddies can protect you from me?'

'Get in the car,' Lisa said. She calmly but firmly grabbed Kirsty's arm and broke her out of the trance. 'NOW!'

Lisa followed Abby and Kirsty into the car. She pressed the central-locking button just as Charlie's palms slammed against the rear passenger window making all three women scream.

'Drive,' said Abby, as Lisa fumbled with the keys, trying to get them in the ignition. 'DRIVE!'

Lisa felt her heart quicken and her hands stiffen. This was her worst nightmare – one of them anyway – coming to life. Her whole life since Frank had been about guarding against something like this, about being ready for anything that might happen to her. Was she going to fail now? Was everything she had put herself through for the last few years going to be for nothing? Charlie had found something hard, a rock, a brick maybe. He hurled it against the window. Lisa heard the glass crack.

No.

That was the single word she thought, saw, even tasted in that moment.

No.

She slid the key into the ignition, turned it, put the car in first and her foot down. In her rear-view mirror she saw Charlie, fists clenched, face red as he screamed after them. Then he ran to his car.

'It's OK, love,' Lisa said, trying to calm Kirsty. 'Take deep breaths.'

'Where's Ray?' Lisa looked for him as they passed the café, but there was no sign of him. 'Do you think he's hurt?'

'We'll find him. But, for now, we need to worry about Charlie,' Abby said, twisting in her seat. 'He's behind us. What should we do? Can you go faster?'

'It's a twenty-mile speed limit!' Lisa said. 'There are speed bumps!'

'Drive to the police station,' Abby said.

'I don't know where it is. Look it up on your phone,' Lisa said as she slowed down at a zebra crossing for a couple of kids and a dog to cross.

'Oh my god, Lisa!' Abby yelled.

'I'm not going to run down children and dogs because of that scumbag!' Lisa said. 'Besides, he's not going to try anything while we are in the middle of town. He knows the police would be here in seconds.'

'It's not that,' Abby said. 'Although also that. My phone, I left it in my jacket in the café. Pass me yours.'

'Mine only does texts and calls!' Lisa said, as she finally got moving again, shifting into second gear.

'Right, well, I'll call the police then!' Abby leant forward, taking Lisa's Nokia from the coffee compartment. 'Christ, it's dead!'

'Plug it into the charger,' Lisa said. 'It should only take a couple of minutes.'

She put her foot down as they headed out of town and towards the moor, but picking up speed didn't make her feel any better. As the town, houses and people slipped away behind them, they drove into wild moorland. And Lisa felt their safety net slip away too. It felt like anything could happen out here. And no one would know.

'Check the phone,' Lisa said, as she heard it beep.

'No signal!' Abby said. 'Bloody Cornwall!'

'He's close,' Lisa said. 'Really close.'

'Maybe try fifth gear?' Abby suggested.

Kirsty sat perfectly still, staring straight ahead, as Lisa pressed her foot down. But it was no good. Her Micra was never going to be faster than Charlie's BMW.

'We aren't going to outrun him,' she said.

'Then just stop,' Kirsty said. 'Just pull over. Let me get out. It's me that he wants. Once he's got me, he'll leave you alone.'

'Are you crazy?' Abby said. 'No way, we never leave a man behind.'

'You barely know me,' Kirsty said. 'I'm a stranger, a no one. I don't matter to anyone. Look, there's a lay-by ahead. Just pull over. I'll get out, and this will be over.'

And then Lisa knew exactly what she had to do.

Slowing down, she indicated as she pulled into the lay-by.

'Lisa, man! What are you doing?' Abby cried as she came to a stop. 'Don't do this!'

Kirsty pulled at the door, but the child locks on the back doors were on.

'I can't get out,' Kirsty said.

'I know,' Lisa said, watching in her rear-view mirror as Charlie got out of his car. She saw him put on his sunglasses and begin to strut over to them, cock of the walk. Lisa looked from him to the road, empty of traffic as far as the eye could see and back again. 'That's because there is no way on earth that I would ever hand you over to that monster. You do matter, Kirsty. You matter to me, and you matter to Abby and Ray, and your aunt and we are going to sort this out. That prick is not going to win.'

Lisa slammed her foot hard on the accelerator just as Charlie approached. Fighting to control the Micra, she turned hard right onto the road and headed back towards Bodmin. Abby cheered as they watched Charlie scrambling back to his car.

'What are you doing?' Kirsty said. 'This is only going to make him mad!'

'Exactly,' Lisa said, as the Micra sped along. 'And that's exactly how we want him to be.'

'She's got a plan!' Abby whooped. 'I have no idea what it is, but Lisa has gone all Captain Poldark on Charlie's arse!'

Lisa stopped the Micra dead at the same zebra crossing as before and waited. Sure enough, Charlie got out of the car almost at once. This time he was carrying something. A baseball bat.

'Abby, cover her with your coat,' Lisa said. 'Sit tight. OK girls, it's going to be OK.'

Charlie slammed the baseball bat into her windscreen. The glass cracked and buckled but did not give way. Kirsty screamed and cried, and Abby swore, hard and loud, but Lisa didn't move. She just watched him, waiting. Another blow landed on the front passenger-door window, and then he smashed her lights front and back. He didn't see the crowd gathering, the people making phone calls, hopefully to the police, taking videos and photos. Lisa watched him, perfectly calmly. And she knew that the calmer she was, the more angry he would get.

Finally he stood at her window, his sunglasses gone, his face twisted and angry as he raised the bat.

'I'm going to fucking kill you, bitch,' he screamed.

'I don't think so, son,' the police officer said, slamming him hard against the car, grabbing the baseball bat and then putting him on the floor.

'Yes! Yes!' Abby cheered. 'Go the feds! Fuck that! Go Lisa, you are one ice-cold, crazy hard case.'

Lisa waited until Charlie was handcuffed and in the back of a police car.

It was only when she got out that she realised her legs were trembling so hard that she could barely stand.

'You all right, love?' A woman police officer rushed to support her.

'Yes,' Lisa said. 'I think we are. Where's Ray? Is he OK?'

'Oh yes, Ray. Yes, he came to the station a few minutes ago. He's got a bloody nose, but he's being checked out and he seems OK.'

'Thank God.' Lisa felt a rush of relief.

'Want to tell us what's been going on?' the young woman asked her.

'Yes,' Lisa said. 'It's a very long story.'

Much later, as WPC Grey passed her a statement to sign, Lisa said, 'I'm sorry. What a mess.'

'Look,' WPC Grey said, 'I'm not going to say that I think the public should get involved with this sort of thing. *But*, if your story checks out – if the things you say about this Charlie are true, and I've met his sort before – well, you and your friends rescued a child from harm. You brought her back to her family, and helped bust a major child-abuse ring. I don't think you should apologise for that, do you? It took a lot of courage to do what you did today. You're one brave woman.'

One brave woman.

She's talking about me, Lisa thought. That's me she's talking about.

CHAPTER NINE

∗∗∗∗∗∗∗∗∗∗∗∗∗∗∗∗∗∗∗∗∗∗∗∗∗

Location: Yeast of Bodmin

Radio station: NBC Radio

Track playing: 'All By Myself' by Celine Dion

Miles travelled: feels like a million

Miles until Captain Poldark: still 4

'Are you sure you're OK?' Ray asked, pouring them another strong cup of tea.

Lisa nodded, 'I am. Can't say the same for my car. Or your poor face.'

'I'm OK,' Ray said, briefly touching his taped-up nose. 'He just threw a lucky punch . . .'

'Mate,' Abby said, 'your car died a hero's death.'

'I think it's more critically injured,' Ray said. 'I think it's mostly on the surface. She'll be on the road again in a few days maybe. In the meantime we're in Bodmin. Kirsty's with her aunt. Social services and the police are taking care of that scumbag. And it's only four in the afternoon. Shall we go and find Captain Poldark?'

'How?' Lisa said. 'No car? A bus maybe, but you never know what kind of nutters you might meet on a bus . . .'

'You might meet us, for starters,' Abby said.

Ray held up a set of keys.

'Alison lent me her van, said it was the least she could do,' Ray said, holding up a set of keys and nodding at a battered old Jeep. 'Come on, people. This mission is not over.'

'Copy that,' Abby said.

'Well, maybe it's not too late,' Lisa said, with a faint smile. 'We'll never know unless we try.'

✦

The crew were still there, sorting things out after a day of filming that had begun at dawn. But the lights in the trailers were out and the word was that the cast had left about half an hour earlier. A small crowd of onlookers were still gathered, wrapped in blankets, with flasks of tea. They watched as the crew took down the lighting and packed away the catering. But any chance of finding Captain Poldark here had gone.

'We were soooo close,' Abby said. 'It's like I can still smell his sweat in the air.'

She inhaled deeply, and Ray and Lisa exchanged a look.

'We've got to see all this,' Lisa said. 'This is quite exciting.'

'This is like turning up at Glastonbury when everyone else has gone home,' Abby said.

'Well, this isn't the only location,' Ray said. 'They're filming again tomorrow, and the day after that. I was chatting to one of the riggers. She used to be in my regiment. We didn't find Captain Poldark today, but we will find him tomorrow. I promise.'

Lisa smiled and walked away from the little crowd of spectators, feeling a sudden need to be alone. The landscape unfolded before her and she stood, with the wind in her hair, looking out at miles and miles of heather trembling in the breeze. The thought struck her that for so long now, she had felt lonely, terrified, lost and trapped. And yet now, she knew she was OK. More than that, she knew that she could be alone and she would be OK. And she knew something else too . . . she could be with other people and still be OK.

'What's a pretty maid like 'ee be doing out 'ere?'

Lisa turned round to find Ray in his full Captain Poldark costume, with the scar on the right side of his face this time. He still looked ridiculous.

'Oh my word,' she said, chuckling. 'What *are* you doing?'

'Well, I knew you wanted to find Captain Poldark out here tonight, and I knew you were let down so I thought at the very least I'd give you a laugh.'

Lisa smiled and took a step closer to him.

'Do you know what?' she said. 'I'm not let down at all. Because I found him. I found Captain Poldark. Or at least the spirit of him. I found him here, in the wind and the land. And here. In my heart. I was flipping hard as nails today. I was brave. I *was* Captain Poldark. I don't need an imaginary hero to keep me safe, and make me feel OK about the world. I just need me. I am Captain Poldark.'

Ray looked deep into Lisa's eyes. For one dizzying moment she thought he might kiss her, and she thought she might like it. Then he checked himself, as Abby sniffed loudly near to them.

'I think you'll find that I'm Captain Poldark,' he said, smiling.

'Er, no,' Abby said, as she joined them, shouting into the wind. 'I'm Captain Poldark!'

'Actually,' Ray said suddenly, 'I think you'll find that's *his* job.'

Lisa and Abby looked to where he was pointing. A brooding, familiar figure appeared over the ridge, sweat sheening his bronzed skin.

'Um, hello,' Lisa said.

'All right, mate,' Ray called.

'Please may I lick you?' Abby said.

Captain Poldark, or Aidan Turner, raised his three-cornered hat in greeting before striding away across the moor to the crew who were waiting for him.

'That is one very gorgeous and talented Aidan Turner,' Lisa whispered under her breath, 'but *I* am Captain Poldark.'

She began to laugh and once she started, she couldn't stop.

CHAPTER TEN

* *

Location: 23 (a) Parker Street, Leeds
Radio station: Heart FM
Track playing: 'I Got You Babe' by UB40
Miles travelled: 0
Miles until Captain Poldark: 0

'So, what's new?' Lisa asked Abby when she telephoned a few days after the trip.

'Quite a lot actually,' Abby said. 'I was telling my brother – you know the one that isn't a dick – about our trip and about how I wished I was closer to Mum. Well, we went to see her together. It was OK. I mean it was like really awkward. I talked too much, and she didn't talk much at all and I thought it was all going to go wrong, again. But then at the end, she hugged me, really hard. And she said, I'll see you next week, love. So that's new.'

'Abby, that's great!' Lisa said, as she paced up and down her flat, her stomach knotted with tension. Eventually she paused by the window, pulling back her curtain to peer down the street.

'And what about you? It's today, right?'

'Yes, any second actually.'

'Excited?'

'Terrified,' Lisa confessed.

'No need to be. When you're basically SAS-level trained like me, you learn to read people. And I can tell you . . . that one, he's one of the good ones. And gingers make the best lovers. That's fact.'

The doorbell rang. Lisa made her excuses, hung up and ran down the stairs to the front door. And then she stopped, wondering about what might be waiting for her on the other side. What might happen if she opened the door, she thought? Maybe things that might hurt, or things that might make her sad or scared. But just as likely things that might make her happier than she'd ever been, things that would bring her joy, hope and a future full of promise. She'd learned a lot from watching Kirsty find the courage to start a new life with her family in Cornwall. And from Abby, who got up each day determined to let nothing frighten her.

All of those things waited for her on the other side of the front door, and if she opened it she'd be letting them all in. Good as well as bad.

'Life,' Lisa said. 'Life is waiting for me on the other side of the door, and it's about time I lived it.' She slid back the bolts and flung the door open.

'Hello, Ray,' she said.

'Lisa,' he said. 'Look, the thing is, I haven't stopped thinking about you and I'd really like the chance to get to know you and . . .'

'I know,' Lisa said, taking him by the hand and pulling him into her arms. 'Me, too.'

And as they kissed on the doorstep in that quiet street in Leeds, it felt as if the wild wind was blowing in off the sea, surrounding them. And as if miles of beautiful Cornish landscape was stretching out all around them as far as the heart could see. Because, at last in each other's arms, they both felt at home.

Read on for an extract from Rowan Coleman's
powerful new novel

THE SUMMER OF IMPOSSIBLE THINGS

If you could change the past, would you?

Thirty years ago, something terrible happened to Luna's
mother. Something she's only prepared to reveal
after her death.

Now Luna and her sister have a chance to go back to
their mother's birthplace and settle her affairs. But in
Brooklyn they find more questions than answers, until
something impossible – magical – happens to Luna,
and she meets her mother as a young woman back
in the summer of 1977.

At first Luna's thinks she's going crazy, but if she can
truly travel back in time, she can change things. But in
doing anything – everything – to save her mother's life,
will she have to sacrifice her own?

'Why, sometimes I've believed as many as six impossible things before breakfast.'

Through the Looking Glass, *Lewis Carroll*

PROLOGUE

OXFORDSHIRE, 6 JUNE 2007

Watching my mother's face for the first time since the night she died, I am altered. I am unravelled and undone - in one instant becoming a stranger in my own skin.

There is a theory that just by looking at something you can transform the way it behaves; change the universe and how it works at quantum level, simply by seeing. The observer effect, we call it in physics, or the uncertainty principle. Of course the universe will do what the universe always does, whether we are watching or not, but these are the thoughts I can't shake out of my head as I watch my mother's fragile image, flickering as it's projected on the wall. That just by looking at this film of her, I have changed the fabric of everything I thought I knew.

Just seconds ago my mother told me and my sister that my dad – the man I grew up with, and whom I love – is not my biological father. Yes, the universe around me shifted and reformed for ever; and yet the second she said it I understood that I have always known it to be true, always felt my incongruity, in every beat of my heart, tilt of my head. In my outsider's blue eyes.

There is no choice now but to watch on: the course is set and I am travelling it. I have to see, no matter what, although looking will change everything. It's simple physics, the mystery of the universe encapsulated in these intimate pivotal moments.

But there is no equation to express how I feel, looking at the face of the woman I have missed every second for the last eight months.

She sits in the Oxfordshire country garden of the house I grew up in. The same garden is in full and glorious bloom outside the creaking barn door now, the roses still bear the scars from her pruning, the azaleas she planted are still in bud. But the garden I am watching her sit in may as well be on Mars, so far away from me does she seem. She is so far away now, out of reach for good. A light-grey, cotton dress blows against her bare brown legs, her hair is streaked with silver, her eyes full of light. There's an old chair from the kitchen, its legs sinking slightly into the soft grass. This must have been recorded in late summer because the rhododendron bushes are in bloom, their dark glossy leaves reflecting the sun. It was probably last summer, just after Dad got the all clear, after a few terrifying weeks in which we thought he might have bowel cancer. That means that as long ago as last summer, months and months before she died, she knew already what she was going to do. I experience this realisation as a physical pain in my chest, searing and hot.

'Although the watch keeps ticking on my wrist ... ' her captured image is saying, the breeze lifting the hair off her face, 'I am still trapped back there, at least part of me is. I'm pinned like a butterfly to one single minute, in one single hour, on the day that changed my life.'

There are tears in her eyes.

'To everyone around me it might have seemed that I kept walking and talking, appearing to be travelling through time at the allotted sixty seconds per minute, but actually I was static, caught in suspended animation, thinking, always thinking about that one act ... that one ... choice.'

Her fingers cover her face for a moment, perhaps trying to cover the threat of more tears, her throat moves, her chest stills. When her hands fall back down to her lap she is smiling. It's a smile I know well: it's her brave smile.

'I love you, my beautiful daughters.'

It's a phrase that she had said to us almost every day of our lives, and to hear her say it again, even over the thrum of the projector, is something like magic, and I want to catch it, hold it in the palm of my hand.

Leaning forward in her chair, her eyes search the lens, searching me out, and I find myself edging away from her, as if she might try to reach out and touch me.

'I made this film as my goodbye, because I don't know when – or if – I will have the courage to say it in person. It's my goodbye, and something else. It's a message for you, Luna.'

When she says my name, I can feel her breath on my neck as she speaks.

'The truth is, I don't know if I ever want to you see it, to see any of this. Perhaps you never will. Perhaps here, in this moment, in this way, is the only time I can tell you and Pia about my other life, the life I live alongside the one I have with you girls and your father, the life I live in a parallel universe, where the clock's second hand never moves forward. Yes, I think ... I think this is the only place I'm brave enough to tell you.' She shakes her head, tears glisten, whilst behind her head the ghosts of long dead bees drone in and out of the foxgloves, collecting pollen over the brickwork of a derelict building.

'You see, once, a long time ago, something really, really bad happened to me, and I did something terrible in return. And ever since that moment, there has been a ghost at my shoulder, following me everywhere I go, waiting everywhere I look, stalking me. And I know, I know that one day I won't be able to outrun him any more. One day he will catch up with me. One day he will have his revenge. One day soon. If you are watching this,' her voice hooks into me, 'then he already has me ... '

She draws so close to the lens that we can only see one unfocused quarter of her face; she lowers her voice to a whisper. 'Listen, if you look very hard and very carefully you'll find me in Brooklyn, in the place and the moment I never truly left. At our building, the place I grew up in, that's where you will find me, and the other films I made for you. Luna, if you look hard enough – if you want to look after you know what I did … He wouldn't let me go, you see. Find me … please.'

7 JULY 2007

'*This distinction between past, present, and future is only an illusion.*'

—Albert Einstein

CHAPTER ONE

* *

We travel in a kind of bubble, my little sister Pia and I, sheltered in the quiet, cool interior of an air-conditioned cab, while outside the searing summer streets of an unfamiliar landscape unfold ever outwards as we make each turn. We slip past bridges and buildings that are a kind of second-hand familiar, the relics of the tales which we grew up listening to; a constantly increasing map of a world neither of us have ever visited before, but which is written into our DNA.

Bay Bridge, Brooklyn, is nothing like I imagined it would be after a lifetime of watching movies set in New York State. It's a low, two-storey landscape of wide avenues and neat, wooden-clad houses; small town America, on the edge of a huge borough that lives right next door, the greatest city on earth. New York seems to peer at Bay Ridge over the expanse of the Hudson with an uninterested shrug.

There is an air of quiet certainty unfurling in the searing July sunshine. Even the people meandering down the sidewalks have an innately serene look about them, as if this place is made only for them, a safe place, a place where the rest of the world never looks, a place where secrets might never be discovered if you know where to hide them. This is where life and love and death can quietly play out, without barely making a ripple of the surface of the planet. It's almost as if when you cross the Brooklyn Bridge times slows down just a little, right at its zenith.

This is the world where our mother grew up, the world she ran away from, never to return. It never occurred to us that one day it would be us travelling back here, all the way back to her starting point. Officially we are here to finally settle her estate, and begin the sale of the long derelict, boarded-up building she co-owned with her sister, a woman she hadn't spoken to in thirty years. The building had once been her home, the centre of her universe. Unofficially, secretly, we came because she told us to. To look for her, and to look for clues about my biological father, whose existence still seems like a mangled dream to me.

'She could have just got it wrong,' Pea had said after the film ended, disturbed dust still settling in the light of Dad's projector that we'd had to borrow in secret. 'I mean, in her darkest moment, she had delusions. She had fantasies. She could have just been living a nightmare out loud, that could be it.'

'Yes,' I said, slowly, uncertainly, letting her words seeps into me through every pore. 'Yes, it could be that ... but ... '

I looked at my sister, and I knew she was beginning to see what I already knew. My bright blue eyes, the only blues eyes for generations on either side of the family, as far back as anyone can remember.

'But you have to find out if it might be true,' Pea finished for me. 'They loved each other so much, especially back then, when she left Brooklyn, left her family to be with him. It just doesn't make sense that there would be another man ... But even if there was, it doesn't change anything. You're still you. You're still our Luna.'

She couldn't know that I had always felt a little bit like a stranger in my own family, a little bit out of step with them. That, somehow, what Mum said was strangely comforting.

Dad had wanted to come on this trip, but we'd persuaded him to stay at home. Even now, months later, he was so fragile after losing her, his blood pressure still high, and the doctor didn't recommend flying. We didn't tell about the film, even though we could have. We could have asked him outright if it was true, and taken him at his word, but we didn't. It seemed too cruel for him to lose a wife and a daughter in the space of a few months, even if we loved each other in just the same way as we always have. I think him knowing that I knew would hurt him. So we begged him to stay at home, be taken care of by his friends, and let us sort out the paperwork. And maybe uncover secrets, and part of me. The part of me that was most like my mother, truly believed she might be waiting there for us.

Her sister, Stephanie, had wanted to sell the minute their father, our grandfather, had died in 1982. Lawyers' letters came in the post thick and fast; and although I didn't really know what they were about, I could see how just the sight of the distinctive airmail envelope would make my mother's hands tremble. Mum had refused to sell, she wouldn't budge. She had her reasons, we never knew them, but whatever they were, perhaps she planned it this way, because she had left her half of her family home to Pea and I. And now – just when we need it – there is money waiting to be accessed. One trip to Bay Ridge, put the building on the market, and there should be enough from the proceeds to get my sister back on her feet, this time for good. And perhaps I can find answers to questions I've always had, even if I haven't quite known what they were.

Pea – I've called her that since she was born – sits nervously, her fingers twitch in her lap, her nails are broken and bitten down, knuckles pinks and grazed, with combat, but not a fist fight. These are the scars of her daily battle not to reach for a drink or a pill. Twenty-four years old and eight weeks clean this time. Last time she stayed sober for eighteen months, and I thought maybe she had cracked it, but then Mum died, suddenly and shockingly. I fought so hard to hold on to her, against the tsunami of grief and chaos that we could both see was coming to sweep her away, but I wasn't strong enough.

This time I won't let my sister down.

This time, I will keep her safe. If I can just hold on to what matters, what is *real*, then I will be able to save her.

Resting the weight of my camera on my thigh, I reach out and take her hand, stilling it. She looks at me from behind the pink, heart-shaped sunglass she bought at the airport.

'What did you bring that old thing for, anyway?' she asks me, nodding at the camera, my dad's old Pentax, the one he was looking through the very first time he set eyes on Mum. 'You couldn't even get fifty quid for it on eBay. I know, because I tried once. It's all digital now, you know.'

'I know, but this is more than just a camera it's a … relic. It's a little piece of Mum and Dad's story, and besides, I like looking at things through a lens. I thought I could shoot the places that Dad shot, recreate the images for him. He might not have been up to making the trip but his camera could, I thought he'd like it.'

'He will like it,' Pea nods. 'You should have been a photographer, not a scientist, you're too artistic to be a scientist.'

'I'm a physicist,' I remind her. 'And actually a lot of what I do is art. How are you feeling?'

'Like I'd really like a drink, a hit or both,' she says. 'But then again, I'm awake, so nothing new there.'

We let the road slip under us in silence for a few moments.

'But how are you?' she asks finally. 'I mean *really*.'

I hesitate, if I were to answer that question accurately I'd say full of rage and grief, terrified and lost, unsure and unable to find a sure-footed place to stand. But I don't. Our beloved mother died from an overdose, and, even after a lifetime of a family that revolved around her depression, we didn't see it coming in time to save her, and I can't forgive myself for that. And more than that, there's a stranger inside me, a stranger who *is* me, a crucial part of me I don't have any reference for, and that unnerves me.

'I think it will be a challenging few days, being here without her,' I say instead, choosing my words carefully. 'I'd always thought we'd come back here one day all together, you, me, Mum and Dad. I always thought there would be an end, like a resolution, and she'd be better, be happy. I never thought the ending would be that she'd ... '

'Kill herself,' Pea finishes.

'Christ.' I bow my head, the now familiar surge of sickening guilt rises in my throat, that I didn't see what she was about to do. 'How can it be real? How can that be what's really happened? I didn't see it coming. I should have seen it coming. I should have ... but she seemed, better, brighter. Free. I relaxed, I shouldn't have relaxed.'

'Maybe it's better that you didn't,' Pea says. 'That *we* didn't.'

'Pia, how can you say that?'

'Because. Because it wore her out, all that effort at being happy. For our whole childhood, painting on smiles just for us and Dad. She was exhausted by it, but she saw it through, because she loved us. I'd been clean for more than a year, you'd got your doctorate, and were going to move in with Brian. Dad was through the cancer scare. Don't you think she finally thought that now we were all OK, she could just go? Just stop feeling the pain, and go. Don't you think that's why she seemed happier? The end was in sight.'

I don't know how to answer, so I don't speak.

'Seen Brian?' Pea changes the subject with ease, from one thing I can't bear to talk about to another.

'No,' I shake my head. 'I'm glad I haven't seen him. He isn't the sort of person you want to see when you're … conflicted.'

Pea snorts. 'Conflicted. Yep, our mum tops herself and we're "conflicted". I take it back, you are the perfect scientist – analytical to the last.' The spasm of hurt her words cause must show on my face, because she takes off her glasses, and leans into me. 'You know I don't mean it,' she says. 'And, anyway, it was a good job you found out what a flake Brian was before you ended up marrying him. It's good to know if someone will be willing to stick by you in a crisis. And he, well … you know.'

I do know. I'd discovered Brian was on a minibreak in the Lake District with another woman on the day of Mum's funeral. It should hurt me more than it does; after all, we'd been together for two years and talked about making it official. But somehow I am numb to that petty betrayal. It took me leaving Brian to realise that, as much as I liked him, and respected him, I was never in love with him, and he knew that. When I think back, I doubt that he was ever in love with me either, it was more that I fascinated him, I was atypical, an anomaly and as a neuroscientist he liked that about me. I was a woman immersed in the most rational of sciences, determined that my sex wasn't going to hold me back, even when most of the rest of the world I moved in was.

I can see, now, the reason I was drawn to him was because I thought he understood me. I thought he was like me, but that was a mistake. It wasn't our similarities that he enjoyed about me; it was our differences that he liked to study.

It probably didn't help that I told him my secret. I shouldn't have told him. That just after Mum died something started happening to me that hadn't happened since I was a little girl. That sometimes, more and more just recently, I see things; people, places ... things.

Impossible things. Things that are not there.

About Quick Reads

Quick Reads are brilliant short new books written by bestselling writers. They are perfect for regular readers wanting a fast and satisfying read, but they are also ideal for adults who are discovering reading for pleasure for the first time.

Since Quick Reads was founded in 2006, over 4.5 million copies of more than a hundred titles have been sold or distributed. Quick Reads are available in paperback, in ebook and from your local library.

To find out more about Quick Reads titles, visit

www.readingagency.org.uk/quickreads

Tweet us 🐦 @Quick_Reads

Quick Reads is part of The Reading Agency, a national charity that inspires more people to read more, encourages them to share their enjoyment of reading with others and celebrates the difference that reading makes to all our lives.
www.readingagency.org.uk Tweet us @readingagency

The Reading Agency Ltd · Registered number: 3904882 (England & Wales) Registered charity number: 1085443 (England & Wales) Registered Office: Free Word Centre, 60 Farringdon Road, London, EC1R 3GA The Reading Agency is supported using public funding by Arts Council England.

We would like to thank all our funders:

Discover the pleasure of reading with Galaxy®

Curled up on the sofa,
Sunday morning in pyjamas,
just before bed,
in the bath or
on the way to work?

Wherever, whenever,
you can escape
with a good book!

So go on...
indulge yourself with
a good read and the
smooth taste of
Galaxy® chocolate.

Proudly supports Quick Reads

 **has something for everyone**

Stories to make you laugh

Stories to make you feel good

Stories to take you to another place

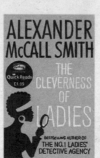 

Stories about real life

Stories to take you to another time

Stories to make you turn the pages

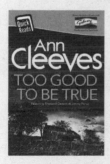

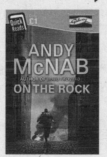

For a complete list of titles visit

www.readingagency.org.uk/quickreads

Available in paperback, ebook
and from your local library

Start a new chapter

One False Move

Dreda Say Mitchell

Hayley swore when she got out of prison that
she would turn her life around.

But living on the Devil's Estate doesn't make that easy.

She spends her days looking after her daughter, and her nights
collecting cash from people who can't get loans any other way.

But someone has just robbed her. And she has twenty-four
hours to get the money back, or her boss will come for her.

Her criminal ex-boyfriend says he can help.
Hayley wants nothing to do with him. But time is running out,
and she has to choose – save herself, or save her soul?

If she makes one false move, her life will be over . . .

Available in paperback, ebook and from your local library

Start a new chapter

The Other Side of You

Amanda Craig

Will must run, or die. He's seen a murder,
and the gang on his estate are after him.

Hurt, hungry and afraid, he comes to an abandoned house in
a different part of the city. Behind its high fences is a place of
safety. Here, he can hide like a wounded beast. He can find
food, and healing – and learn how to do more than survive.

But when Will meets Padma, he must choose between his good
side and his bad one. For the gang he left behind is still there.
How can he live without becoming a killer?
How can he love without being a thief?

Exciting, fast-paced and different, this is a story
that keeps you reading until the last line.

Available in paperback, ebook and from your local library

A Very Distant Shore

Jenny Colgan

**Wanted: doctor for small island. Must like boats,
the seaside and having no hope of keeping a secret ...**

Lorna lives on the tiny Scottish island of Mure,
a peaceful place where everyone helps their neighbour.
But the local GP is retiring, and nobody wants his job.
Mure is too small and too remote.

Far away, in a crowded camp, Saif is treating a little boy
with a badly-cut hand. Saif is a refugee, but he's
also a doctor: exactly what Mure needs.

Saif is welcome in Mure, but can he forget his past?
Over one summer, Saif will find a place to call home,
and Lorna's life will change forever.

Available in paperback, ebook and from your local library

Why not start a reading group?

If you have enjoyed this book, why not share your next Quick Read with friends, colleagues, or neighbours?

The Reading Agency also runs **Reading Groups for Everyone** which helps you discover and share new books. Find a reading group near you, or register a group you already belong to and get free books and offers from publishers at **readinggroups.org**

There is a free toolkit with lots of ideas to help you run a Quick Reads reading group at **www.readingagency.org.uk/quickreads**

Share your experiences of your group on Twitter

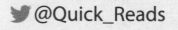 @Quick_Reads

Continuing your reading journey

As well as Quick Reads, The Reading Agency runs lots of programmes to help keep you and your family reading.

Reading Ahead invites you to pick six reads and record your reading in a diary to get a certificate **readingahead.org.uk**

World Book Night is an annual celebration of reading and books on 23 April **worldbooknight.org**

Chatterbooks children's reading groups and the **Summer Reading Challenge** inspire children to read more and share the books they love **readingagency.org.uk/children**